# ⋟LOOK AT THIS!⋞
# CLOTHES

## Ifeoma Onyefulu

**F**

FRANCES LINCOLN
CHILDREN'S BOOKS

# Shorts

# INTRODUCTION

Ever since I was a child in Nigeria, learning about other African countries, I dreamt about visiting the beautiful country of Mali and seeing its rich culture. So this is where I have chosen to photograph my new word book, *Clothes*.

In Mali, as in most African countries, people wear Western and traditional clothes, and sometimes they combine the two or make Western clothes using African prints. In my book you'll find some children dressed in Western clothes – shorts, dress, t-shirt, and others in traditional clothes – headscarf and wrapper. And sometimes children wear Western and African clothes. Look out for the girl in a hat and an African print top, and another with beads in her hair, wearing a dress. I also wanted to show some traditional Malian clothes, so I took photographs of a man in *bou-bou*, another in a cap – *un bonnet* – and a woman in *Bogolan* dress.

*Bou-bou* is a long, flowing gown worn by men in Mali. It is very comfortable and it can be worn for going out or relaxing at home.

The *Bogolan* dress, light and very comfortable, is made from mud-painting – Mali is full of artists – and this was my way of paying homage to the women mud-painters I met on my travels. The *Bogolan* dress can be worn at any time.

I want to introduce my young readers to the kinds of clothes children in Mali wear, at home and on special occasions such as the Muslim festival of Eid.

It was a great honour for me to create this book. I enjoyed every moment of it and I hope my photographs have truly captured the Malian sense of style.

# Long skirt and a top

# T-shirt

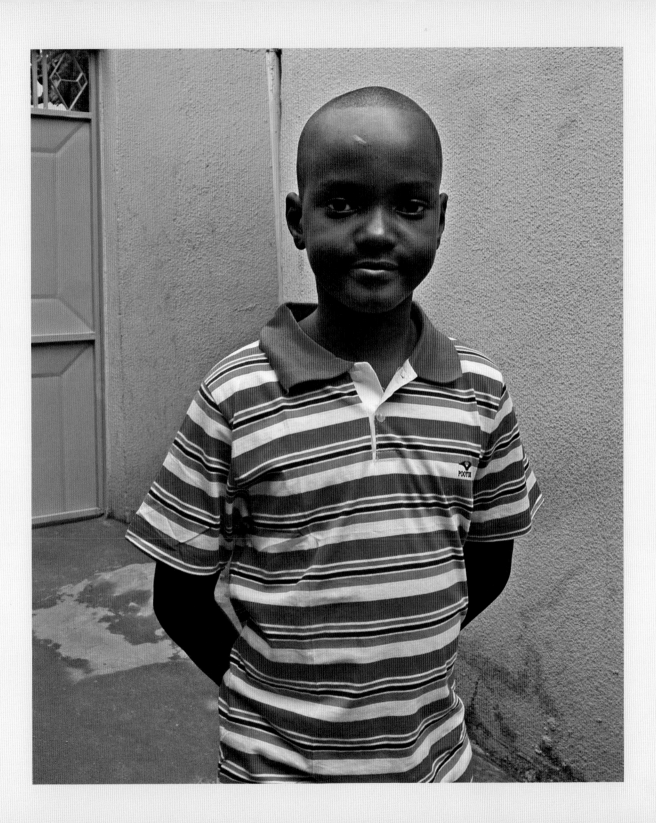

# Scarf

# Dress

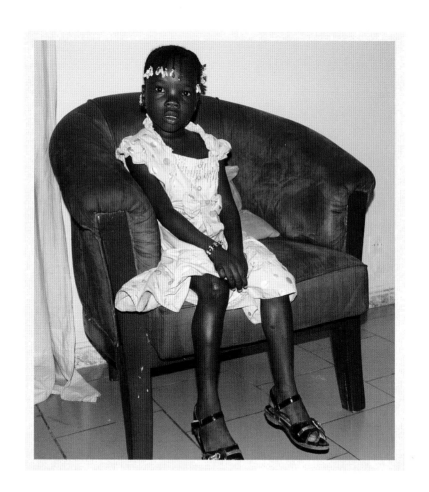

# Trousers

# Shoes

# Bou-bou

(a traditional robe)

# Hat

Cap

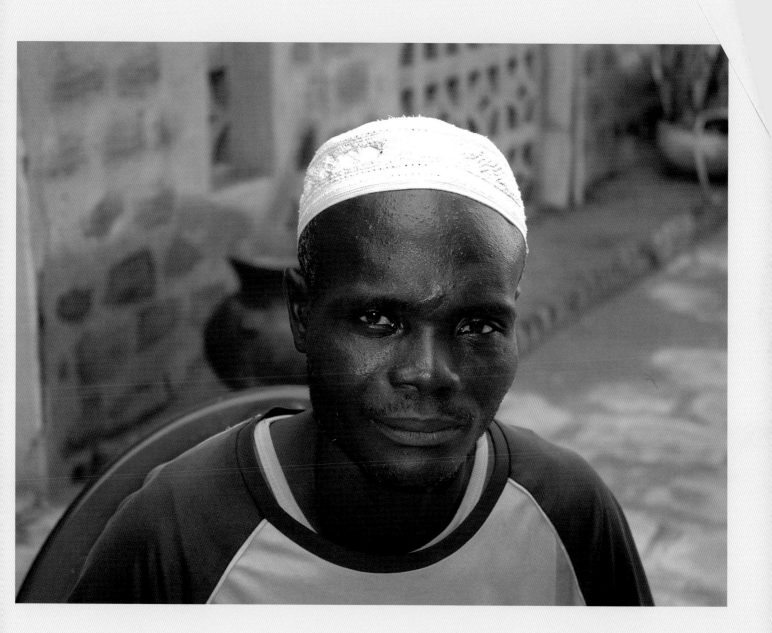

# Wrapper

# Bogolan Dress

(a dress made from traditional printed fabric)

To my lovely sister Chinye, Dr. Ouassa Sanogo
and to Sue and Tim for their support over the years.

JANETTA OTTER-BARRY BOOKS

First published in Great Britain and in the USA in 2012 by
Frances Lincoln Children's Books, 4 Torriano Mews,
Torriano Avenue, London NW5 2RZ
www.franceslincoln.com

A catalogue record for this book is available from the British Library.

ISBN 978-1-84780-264-4

Set in Plantagenet Cherokee

Printed in Dongguan, Guangdong, China by Toppan Leefung in May, 2012

1 3 5 7 9 8 6 4 2